Published by Carte Blanche Greetings Ltd

Carte Blanche Greetings Ltd
PO Box 500
Chichester
PO20 2XZ
UK

www.carteblanchegreetings.com

First Published 2003

ISBN 0-9544951-0-1

1 3 5 7 9 10 8 6 4 2

Printed in Belgium by Proost

British Library Cataloguing in Publication Data is available

To find out more about Me to You visit the web site at:
www.metoyou.co.uk

A Grey Bear with a Blue Nose ?

The Me to You Story

by Miranda
Illustrated by Steve Mort-Hill

The oldest, smallest house you can imagine
was about to be knocked down.

All the things that once made the house nice and cosy had been thrown outside and piled up in the front garden, from the soft springy bed the owners slept in, to the old wooden floorboards they used to walk on…

…and even,
surely by some mistake…
…a little brown teddy bear.

He was trapped amongst all the
other unwanted things, and couldn't move.

Then, one day…a very, very cold day, something
fell from the sky…

…a little snowflake.

It landed on the teddy bear's little nose and was then followed by many more.

He began to get cold, very cold indeed.

More and more snow fell,
heavier and heavier.
The little bear was now so cold
that his nose started turning blue…

…so cold that his brown fur started turning grey.
He was cold, unloved and all alone in the world,

and felt very, very sad.

Winter finally passed and the weather got warmer.
Then, one beautiful spring day, a little girl was
playing near the old house, when she
spotted the grey bear in the pile of
unwanted things.

He was like no other bear she had ever seen…

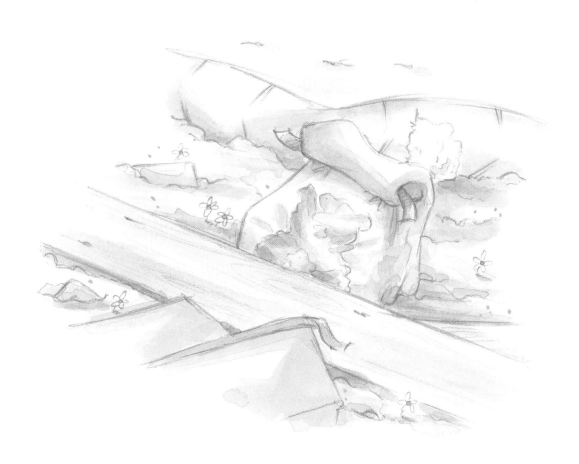

…and she pulled him out from where he was trapped.

She dusted him down and lifted him high in the sky to look at him.

"A grey bear…with a blue nose?" she thought. "How strange!"

The teddy bear wanted to cry. He thought she didn't like him and would throw him back with the other unwanted things.

"But he's lovely!" she continued and she fell completely in love with him.

She ran home as fast...

...as her little legs would carry her...

…to see if her Grandma could patch him up…

...as a lot of his stuffing had fallen out,
and he was very much in need of repair.

She looked on as her Grandma replaced his
stuffing and patched up his holes.

His stitches had started showing where the
fur had worn away, but the little girl thought
he looked perfect.

It was all cosy and warm in the little girl's house and the bear now felt cosy and warm in his heart. However, his nose was still blue and his fur was still grey, and they would never return to brown. He was unique amongst teddy bears.

The little girl gave him a great big hug. She loved him more than anything else in the world…her little, grey, blue-nosed…

…tatty teddy.